About the Author:

Elliot Hargrave is a postgrad researcher in *Engineering Physics* who writes occasionally to decompress from the chaos of academia. When not buried in equations, simulations, or the ever-growing pile of literature reviews, Elliot takes a break by examining the absurd and amusing clashes between STEM and the humanities.

Writing offers Elliot a creative outlet to poke fun at the academic world, from the rigid logic of engineering to the fluid musings of social sciences. His work often reflects the strange dissonance he observes while balancing the technical with the abstract, combining humor with a touch of irreverence.

Outside of research, Elliot enjoys tinkering with gadgets, reading about niche topics, and imagining what might happen if engineers and sociologists were tasked with designing a bridge (answer: lots of debates, no bridge). With a knack for satire and a love for highlighting contradictions, Elliot hopes to make readers laugh—and maybe think a little—about the world of academia and beyond.

Preface:

Welcome to The Language Barrier: Terminology Differences Between STEM and Sociology, a book that boldly explores the delightful chaos that unfolds when the rigorous world of STEM (Science, Technology, Engineering, and Mathematics) collides with the abstract and fluid realm of sociology. If you've ever found yourself in a conversation with a sociologist, only to leave wondering if you've just been inducted into a secret society of social constructs—don't worry, you're not alone. This book is for anyone who has ever scratched their head while trying to reconcile the "social construct" of race with the solid, data-driven world of engineering, or how engineers measure load-bearing capacity while sociologists measure power dynamics.

In this satirical exploration, we will venture deep into the terminology that divides these two disciplines, using humor, irony, and a touch of exaggeration to unravel the delightful confusion that arises when these worlds meet. Whether you're a hardened engineer, a sociology enthusiast, or someone who simply wants to understand the hilarious disconnect between what is measurable and what is constructed, this book has something for you. But be warned: the content within should not be taken too seriously—unless you find yourself trapped in a heated debate with a sociologist over the epistemological validity of bridges.

Prepare yourself for a tongue-in-cheek journey through the world of social constructs and engineering marvels, where the only thing more confusing than terminology is trying to figure out how these two worlds can coexist—or if they should at all.

Table of Contents

Chapter 1: Why STEM Students Groan at Sociology 101

The Unfathomable World of Human Behavior

The unfathomable world of human behavior is like a black hole—dark, mysterious, and filled with the occasional random object that defies explanation. For STEM students, whose primary interactions typically revolve around equations, lab results, and the occasional existential crisis over a failed experiment, delving into the chaotic realm of sociology can feel like trying to solve a Rubik's Cube blindfolded. One moment you're contently measuring the acceleration of a dropped pen, and the next, you're knee-deep in a conversation about social constructs that makes you question if your lab partner really is a sentient being or just a very advanced algorithm.

For many STEM students, the groans that echo through the halls of Sociology 101 can often be attributed to our deeply ingrained learning styles and preferences. We thrive in structured environments where the only surprises typically involve the occasional jitters from too much caffeine. In sociology, however, the rules are as fluid and variable as the theories they propose and explore. Why do people behave in seemingly irrational ways? Why do they form cliques based on something as trivial as their favorite ice cream flavors? The answers remain elusive, and no one seems to truly know! This overwhelming confusion can be enough to make a physics major contemplate throwing their textbook out the window, if they even manage to grasp the concept of social gravity in the first place. P.S. The concept is indeed easy to understand but lacks the rigor necessary to be widely accepted in the same way as physical laws.

Yet, it's precisely this unpredictability that makes sociology an invaluable tool for STEM majors and professionals alike. Understanding the complexities of human behavior can significantly enhance real-world applications in various fields such as engineering, technology, and product development. Imagine the difference it makes when designing a user interface based on the social behavior and preferences of your target audience instead of relying solely on your intuition about button placement. By acknowledging that people are much more than mere numbers or functions, STEM students and practitioners can learn to create products that truly resonate with the fascinating and often bewildering nature of human psychology. After all, nobody wants to click on a button that looks like a mushroom unless it's a particularly charismatic mushroom that captures their interest and attention. This deeper understanding can lead to more engaging and effective designs that appeal to users on a psychological level.

The language barrier that exists between sociology and STEM is a vast chasm that could easily rival the Grand Canyon. While STEM students are typically immersed in equations and constants, sociology introduces terms like "cultural hegemony" and "structuralism," which sound more like the names of obscure indie bands than genuine concepts worthy of serious discussion. This disconnect often results in a collective eye roll, as if the entire class has suddenly agreed to take a synchronized nap. It is crucial for professors to find effective ways to bridge this gap, perhaps by incorporating more relatable analogies, such as comparing social norms to the laws of thermodynamics—because who wouldn't want to see how social pressure can be as thrilling as entropy? Even more entertaining, let's suggest that we teach the professors some straightforward concepts like toy modeling before diving into experimentation or even delve into statistics (just kidding). Such efforts could transform the learning experience for everyone involved and foster a more engaging dialogue between these distinct fields

Engagement strategies are absolutely critical in maintaining the interest of STEM students in sociology, lest they retreat into the comforting embrace of their calculators or code, finding refuge in the familiar rather than exploring the complexities of human behavior. Faculty members face the daunting task of transforming the seemingly monotonous study of human interactions into a thrilling quest that resembles the excitement of a sci-fi adventure. By integrating group projects that simulate real-life scenarios or employing innovative gamification techniques, educators can effectively harness the competitive spirit inherent in STEM students. Imagine this: a sociology class that takes on the format of a reality TV show, where students compete to analyze social interactions, complete with dramatic music and surprise eliminations to amplify the stakes. Now, that's a class that could elevate the excitement level—if only to distract from the reality that we may never truly comprehend the unfathomable world of human behavior. Additionally, allowing students to choose their topics of analysis, such as the classification of different styles of mathematicians, engineers, scientists, and even businesspeople, could foster a deeper connection to the subject matter. P.S. It's worth noting that we STEM majors tend to be somewhat introverted, so a professor who is overly enthusiastic might not resonate well with us

3

But Where Are the Formulas?

But where are the formulas? This question echoes through the hallowed halls of Sociology 101 like a ghost haunting the dreams of unsuspecting STEM students. Picture this: you've just finished a grueling session of calculus, where the only thing standing between you and a solid GPA was your ability to derive integrals faster than a caffeinated squirrel. Then, you walk into sociology class, and suddenly, the only formula you can find is the one that dictates how many times you can roll your eyes during a lecture about social constructs. Spoiler alert: it's unlimited.

You might be wondering why sociology seems to lack the elegant equations that grace your beloved physics and chemistry textbooks. It's as if the sociologists decided that instead of deriving complex formulas, they'd rather engage in endless discussions about human behavior and societal norms. "Why do people act the way they do?" they ask, while you're frantically searching for x in the equation of societal interaction. If only they'd throw in a quadratic formula or two, perhaps you'd feel more at home instead of feeling like you've wandered into a philosophical debate between two philosophers who just lost their train of thought.

Learning styles play a significant role in this comedic tragedy. STEM students, who typically thrive on structure and logic, find themselves grappling with the abstract and often squishy nature of sociology. It's like trying to solve a Rubik's Cube while blindfolded and standing on one leg. The lectures are filled with terms like "cultural relativism" and "social stratification," which sound suspiciously like spells from a wizarding school, leaving you to wonder if you should have brought your wand instead of your notebook. Meanwhile, your sociology professor enthusiastically gestures about social phenomena as if they're unveiling the secrets of the universe, while you can't help but think, "Where's my graphing calculator?"

Engagement strategies for keeping STEM students interested in sociology often revolve around the promise of real-world applications. "You'll see how sociology affects your everyday life!" they proclaim, but all you can picture is the last time you tried to understand the social dynamics in your lab group. The only real-world application you're interested in is how to apply a statistical analysis to the number of times your lab partner has made an inappropriate joke. If only they could relate social theories to something tangible, like the physics of a coffee spill during an awkward group discussion.

Lastly, let's not forget the impact of faculty teaching styles. Some professors try to bridge the divide by tossing in a few STEM-related examples, only to watch as their students' eyes glaze over like donuts in a pastry shop. Others dive headfirst into theoretical jargon, completely bypassing any hope of engagement. It's a delicate dance, akin to trying to teach a cat to fetch. The struggle is real, and the only formula that seems to emerge is the one that calculates the number of students silently praying for the semester to end. So, as you sit there pondering the absence of formulas, just remember: sometimes laughter is the best equation for survival in the wild world of sociology.

Group Projects: The Real Social Experiment

Group projects in STEM programs often feel like a social experiment gone awry, where the variables are your classmates and the hypothesis is, "Can we actually finish this without someone going rogue?" Picture this: a group of four or five eager minds, all armed with varying degrees of social skills and caffeine consumption. You begin with high hopes, only to realize that collaboration is a fine art that most of us never learned. Instead, we've mastered the "I will do the bare minimum and hope my genius shines through" approach.

As the project unfolds, the dynamics start to resemble a reality TV show. There's the overachiever who insists on doing everything—let's call them Captain Control. They're the type who has a five-minute PowerPoint ready before the group even decides on a topic. Then there's the procrastinator, who shows up ten minutes before the deadline with a half-baked idea and a sheepish grin. You can almost hear the producers whispering, "This is going to be good." Meanwhile, the quiet one sits in the corner, plotting their escape while pretending to take notes. Spoiler alert: they will ultimately become the hero by suggesting a last-minute pivot that saves everyone's grade.

Navigating group projects also means wrestling with diverse learning styles. While some team members flourish with hands-on tasks, others thrive on theoretical discussions, leading to a clash that can only be described as "the battle of the brains." It's like trying to mix oil and water, except the oil is a meticulous planner and the water is a free spirit who insists that "brainstorming" means doodling on the whiteboard while everyone else stares in disbelief. The result? A chaotic blend of ideas that may or may not resemble the original project plan.

Let's not forget the language barrier that often surfaces in these situations. In STEM, we speak in equations and algorithms, while sociology leans heavily on terms like "social construct" and "cultural hegemony." This mix can lead to some hilarious misunderstandings. Imagine trying to explain the concept of social stratification to a group who believes a stratified random sample is just an overly complicated way to choose pizza toppings. Moments like these remind us that we're not just students; we're also linguists trying to bridge an enormous gap in terminology while simultaneously trying to figure out who's bringing the snacks.

Ultimately, group projects act as a microcosm of society, showcasing the best and worst of human interaction. While they can turn into a circus of misunderstandings, miscommunications, and misplaced responsibilities, they also offer valuable lessons. They teach us about compromise, patience, and the importance of not taking ourselves too seriously. So, as you dive into the next group assignment with a mix of dread and anticipation, remember that every awkward moment and laughable mishap is just part of the grand social experiment that is group work in STEM—a lesson in sociology that might just leave you with a story worth telling at your next gathering.

Wow, they lack seriousness! (interacting with the faculty)

Wow, they have no rigor! When it comes to communicating with faculty in the sociology department, it's as if you've stumbled into a room full of people who just realized that social constructs are actually a thing. Picture this: a STEM student walks into class armed with formulas, equations, and a firm belief that the world operates on laws as unyielding as the laws of physics. Suddenly, they're faced with discussions about feelings, social justice, and the importance of safe spaces. It's like expecting a rigorous math problem and ending up with an interpretive dance about privilege.

Trying to engage with sociology faculty can feel like playing a game of charades where you don't know the theme, the rules, or even how to spell your own name. You ask, "What's the hypothesis?" and they respond with a heartfelt monologue about the societal implications of avocado toast. Meanwhile, you're over here wondering why nobody is wearing lab coats and why the only data being discussed is anecdotal evidence from last weekend's coffee shop conversation. For STEM students, this lack of rigor is enough to make them question whether their degree should come with a side of critical thinking and a dash of existential dread.

When it comes to learning styles, sociology professors seem to have a unique approach that can best be described as "free-range pedagogy." They encourage students to explore their thoughts like a toddler in a candy store, often resulting in a chaotic blend of ideas that make perfect sense to them but leave STEM students scratching their heads. For these analytical minds, the absence of structure can be maddening. They yearn for syllabi that read like a scientific paper, complete with methodology, results, and a conclusive discussion. Instead, they find themselves navigating a syllabus filled with terms like "co-constructing knowledge" and "participatory action research," which sound more like a team-building retreat than an academic endeavor.

Real-world applications? Sure, let's talk about them—after all, that's the bridge that connects the lofty sociological theories to the cold, hard reality that STEM students live in. But when faculty suggest that students can apply sociological concepts to their STEM fields by understanding the social dynamics of their lab groups, the STEM crowd collectively rolls their eyes. Because why grapple with the complexities of human interaction when you can just run a regression analysis? The irony is palpable; sociology wants to make students aware of the social world, while STEM students are just trying to keep their sanity intact amidst the chaos of group projects and lab reports.

In the end, the impact of faculty teaching styles on STEM student engagement is nothing short of comedic tragedy. Faculty members often fail to realize that their students are not just there to earn a grade; they want the kind of intellectual rigor that makes them feel like they've conquered the academic equivalent of Everest. But instead, they're left scaling the heights of abstract theories while navigating a minefield of jargon that sounds suspiciously like it was generated by a random word generator. So, in this delightful clash of cultures, STEM students are left to ponder: how do we find rigor in a world that seems to celebrate the absence of it?

Chapter 2: Learning Styles: How STEM Students Approach Sociology

The Science of Learning: If It Ain't Quantifiable, It Ain't Real

In the expansive realm of academia, where STEM students confidently navigate their calculators and codes, sociology often appears as an enigmatic fog. These students, adept at quantifying everything from the gravitational pull of a dropped pencil to the precise pH level of their morning coffee, may find themselves bewildered by sociological concepts that seem to drift in the ether. If something can't be measured, can it truly be real? For many, the answer is a firm no, leading to significant confusion and, at times, an existential crisis as they attempt to assess the social impact of their favorite meme. We can delve into statistical data that contradicts the key points presented in lectures, yet the common response is that data is inherently imperfect. Now, imagine if I, as a STEM student, claimed to have discovered the concept of quantum consciousness through a dream. What would your reaction be? Sure, I could construct a convoluted equation to "support" my argument qualitatively through classification, but it would lack reproducibility. So, one must ask, is it truly real? This analogy highlights the struggle to reconcile the quantitative with the qualitative, urging a deeper exploration of the social dimensions that may not fit neatly into our established frameworks.

Learning styles have become a trending topic in education, yet the idea that one can simply improve learning by adopting a specific style seems as effective as using a rubber band to repair a broken bridge. STEM students, with their preference for data-driven methods, often find humor in concepts like 'visual learners' and 'auditory learners' while enjoying their carefully crafted espressos, reflecting on the absurdity of such classifications. They approach sociology with a different perspective, searching for graphs, charts, and algorithms to analyze social dynamics, eager for an empirical basis amidst the subjective nature of the field. If only the textbook could provide a flowchart to navigate the complexities of human behavior, it might alleviate the uncertainty and caffeine-fueled anxiety of late-night study sessions. While STEM students may initially be enthusiastic about quantifying sociological concepts, the challenge of confronting logical fallacies and convoluted theories can turn the experience into more of a negotiation than an actual discipline. There are many nuances to consider, and although we acknowledge sociology as a valid area of study, it may align more closely with the interests of economists, psychologists, or business students, whose methods resonate more with the human aspects of the subject. Our primary concern with sociology arises from the tone of the instructors and the syllabus, which sometimes seem to dismiss our data-focused rigor, leaving us feeling misunderstood and alienated in the classroom.

Real-world applications of sociology are increasingly relevant in the STEM field, especially when students realize that their future employers may expect them to grasp team dynamics, interpersonal relationships, or the subtleties of office politics. However, as they sit in class, struggling to find a link between social stratification and their renewable energy project, the tension is evident. "Is it possible to quantify social interactions?" one student might ask, while another questions whether there's a formula to predict if a group project will descend into chaos. Some might think they can just navigate tricky situations through instinct, like networking with influential individuals to escape trouble. Others may adopt a more indifferent attitude, feeling that as long as they can innovate and pursue their passions in research and development, they won't worry about being ostracized or bullied in the workplace. The reality is that there isn't a formula for this, and that's part of its charm—similar to the quest for the perfect pizza recipe

The language barrier that exists between STEM and sociology serves as yet another rich source of humor in this ongoing academic tug-of-war. Students immersed in STEM fields, who can easily rattle off complex terms like "asymptotic behavior" and "quantum entanglement" with a sense of confidence, suddenly find themselves confronted with sociological jargon that sounds suspiciously like an elaborate game of Scrabble gone wildly wrong. Concepts such as "habitus" and "dialectical materialism" might as well be spells from an intricate wizarding world, considering the complete lack of clarity they seem to provide. As these STEM students struggle to decode these perplexing terms, they often resort to whimsical and playful interpretations: "So, are we suggesting that social capital is merely a fancy term for 'who you know at the coffee shop'?" At this juncture, one might genuinely wonder if their professors are secretly chuckling at their bewilderment, perhaps enjoying the spectacle of their confusion as they try to navigate this complex academic landscape.

As for engagement strategies to keep STEM students genuinely interested in the field of sociology, let's consider one word: memes. Yes, these ubiquitous and often humorous snippets of internet culture can serve as an exceptional gateway to complex sociological concepts. Faculty members

12

who skillfully incorporate humor, pop culture references, and, of course, the occasional cat video into their lectures may just discover that they have a truly captivated audience. Nothing ignites curiosity quite like discussing the sociological implications of the latest viral TikTok trend, especially when students can easily relate it back to their own experiences in the lab or classroom. Moreover, if professors could find a way to quantify student engagement, they might just uncover that laughter is indeed the most effective teacher, even in disciplines that are often perceived as purely quantitative. Engaging students through relatable content can foster a deeper understanding of sociology while making the learning experience enjoyable.

Why statistics aren't important (it's all about emotions)

In the vast world of academia, where equations move fluidly and algorithms resonate, statistics often take precedence, overshadowing the nuanced realm of emotions. However, in sociology, those numbers can be as disorienting as a sock on a wet floor—unexpectedly slippery and quite unsettling. After all, who needs statistics when the vibrant mess of human feelings is at play? A statistic may reveal that 70% of individuals prefer chocolate over vanilla, yet it overlooks the existential turmoil of the 30% who suddenly realize they may actually favor vanilla. What does that even mean? Sure, we can investigate the 30% further, but suggesting that they are significantly influenced by complex social forces is a leap. Moreover, focusing on this smaller group seems inefficient without deeper exploration. It's perfectly reasonable to gather focus groups, conduct experiments, and then analyze the findings, rather than simply taking a sample of around 1,000 and concluding, "Oh, 30% of 1,000 is 300, so that's sufficient data." That's not how statistics function. Why not work with a focus group of 300 to support your hypothesis with greater rigor? (This observation is based on the undergraduate research I've encountered; I'm not implying that graduate sociologists fall short.)

Imagine a typical sociology class: the professor animatedly discusses data sets and percentages, while STEM students squirm in their seats, longing for the relief of a pop quiz on quantum mechanics. The reality is that emotions are like the hidden ingredient in the sociology equation—they're chaotic, unpredictable, and certainly not quantifiable. When a sociologist states, "People feel this way," a STEM student interprets it as, "This is not a problem solvable by a differential equation." This is where the conflict arises; one group focuses on numerical analysis, while the other navigates the turbulent seas of human emotion, often feeling like they've stepped into a soap opera. Personally, I believe the disconnect with sociologists stems from our tendency to distance ourselves from emotions, as they can introduce bias. Yet, human psychology is complex and subjective; sometimes we are unaware of our own feelings. Many of us even experience emotional dissonance, but these humanities subjects confront us with this uncomfortable reality, making us want to escape.

Let's not overlook the complex terminology of sociology that often leaves STEM majors baffled. Phrases like "cognitive dissonance" and "social construct" can make it feel like you've entered a philosophical discussion rather than a statistics course. It seems sociologists chose to express emotions in a way that resembles a mix of Shakespeare and a therapy session. Meanwhile, STEM students are communicating in the straightforward language of math and science, where clarity is paramount and ambiguity is avoided. This creates a divide that's broader than the gap between a sociologist's preference for qualitative research and a STEM student's appreciation for a straightforward pie chart. Sometimes we even joke about developing a "scientific perspective" to tackle sociological issues instead of relying on the four or five frameworks we are taught. If we're truly engaging in critical thinking, shouldn't we be encouraged to think independently rather than adhering to preset perspectives?

Engagement strategies in sociology often feel like an intricate game of charades, where the main objective is to evoke a range of emotions in STEM students—anything but confusion, which seems to be the default state. Imagine a professor passionately explaining the profound emotional significance of societal norms while STEM students quietly ponder whether they should calculate the odds of actually caring about such abstract ideas. It's a delicate dance of enthusiasm and indifference, with the professor striving to convince a room full of engineers that emotions hold equal importance to hard principles like the laws of thermodynamics. Spoiler alert: they don't, and deep down, most know this. But at least everyone can agree that emotions can serve as a good punchline to lighten the mood. In some classes, a few of us have even ventured to use the mathematical concept of Fermi's paradox alongside our university data to assess the likelihood of seeking a romantic partner instead of focusing solely on becoming more human in an increasingly technical world.

Ultimately, the impact of faculty teaching styles can transform what might otherwise be a dry sociology lecture into an exhilarating emotional rollercoaster, or conversely, a snooze-fest that feels akin to watching paint dry in slow motion. A charismatic professor has the potential to make students feel as if they've unearthed the profound secrets of the universe, igniting their curiosity and passion for learning. In contrast, a monotone delivery could leave them questioning their very life choices and wondering why they even enrolled in the course. So why do statistics seem to hold little significance in the realm of genuine human feelings? Because at the end of the day, no amount of data can truly capture the sheer absurdity and complexity of human experience. Sometimes, it's the emotions and feelings that resonate with us long after the numbers have faded into obscurity. Spoiler alert: many of us already understand this reality, but we often find it difficult to accept it, especially when the instructor is fervently promoting sociology as a 'hard science' that is supposedly tougher and more 'objective' than physics and engineering.

Visual Learners vs. Verbal Vomiters

In the grand arena of academia, where the gladiators wield calculators and occasionally brandish graphs as their weapons, there exists a peculiar and often amusing dichotomy: the visual learners and the verbal vomiters. Visual learners stand as the noble knights of this intellectual battlefield, equipped with vibrant charts, intricate diagrams, and the occasional meme that effortlessly conveys complex sociological concepts in a single glance. These students flourish in environments rich in visuals, absorbing information like a sponge submerged in a vast ocean of PowerPoint presentations. If you aim to truly engage them, simply display a few compelling graphs on the screen and observe as their eyes light up with enthusiasm. They are the ones who can articulate the intricate social construct of reality while simultaneously crafting a detailed mind map that links every theory to a delightful meme featuring a cat. They may even go so far as to write an equation connecting various social constructs and their potential effects for machine learning predictions based on historical data (p.s. this is merely a toy model; typically, we jokingly create these models and then stash them away somewhere they cannot see the light of day), or they might devise elaborate social engineering scenarios and algorithms to play lighthearted pranks on our unsuspecting peers (for instance, social engineering our way into their social media accounts to post humorous memes, or cleverly acquiring their car keys to relocate their vehicles to another block).

On the other hand, there are those who seem to have an infinite reservoir of words, effortlessly turning a short reply into an elaborate discourse. Armed with a thesaurus and an unyielding urge to hear their own voice, they can articulate the subtleties of Durkheim's theories while you find yourself questioning your life decisions. In sociology classes, they

17

monopolize discussions, fervently reciting definitions and concepts as if auditioning for an Oscar in the realm of academic fervor. These individuals fail to understand why anyone might prefer a visual representation of "class conflict" when an extensive dialogue on Marx's critique of capitalism is available. In such scenarios, they are treated as the experts of verbal perplexity; engaging with them feels like deciphering a foreign language. Their delivery is compelling, yet at times, their magnetic communication skills prompt us to wonder if they possess a disquieting gift akin to that of historical figures known for their persuasive power (you know, the guy rejected by an Austrian art school).

For a visual learner, attending a sociology class can feel overwhelming, like being caught in a storm of words. They might find themselves in the back, gripping their colored markers, wishing for a pie chart to save them from the flood of information. It's comparable to trying to savor a gourmet meal while your dinner partner insists on narrating the recipe in detail. The visual learner's patience wears thin; while they grasp the concepts, the way they're presented feels like drowning in a sea of language. They often leave the class with a headache and a desire for a straightforward infographic to encapsulate what they've learned. Sometimes, they pull out their laptops to start creating visualizations that link the ideas, or they simply give in and browse memes instead.

However, it's not all doom and gloom. When the stars align and a savvy professor recognizes the need for balance, magic can happen. Imagine a sociology lecture that seamlessly blends engaging visuals with verbal explanations. The verbal vomiters can share their passionate insights while the visual learners nod along, their brains lighting up like a Christmas tree as they see theories depicted in vibrant colors. This harmonious teaching style not only keeps both camps engaged but also fosters an environment where ideas can flourish without the fear of drowning in a deluge of words or losing sight of the big picture.

In the end, the battle between visual learners and verbal vomiters isn't a war; it's more of a quirky collaboration. Each group has its strengths and weaknesses, and when they come together, they create a tapestry of understanding that makes sociology not just palatable but downright enjoyable for STEM students. So, educators, take heed: the next time you plan your syllabus, remember that a little visual flair can go a long way in bridging the gap between the diagram-loving data crunchers and the eloquent verbalizers. After all, in the great quest for knowledge, a good laugh and a colorful chart can make all the difference.

The "Eureka!" Moment: Finding Sociology in the Lab

The moment you step into your first sociology class, you might feel like you've entered a parallel universe where the laws of physics are replaced by the laws of social interaction. Instead of equations, you're confronted with terms like "social construct" and "cultural relativism," which sound more like the names of obscure indie bands than concepts you need to grasp. As a STEM student, you might find yourself sitting there, squinting at the syllabus, wondering if you accidentally enrolled in a seminar on existential crises instead of a legitimate academic subject. But hold on to your lab coats, because there's a chance you could experience a "Eureka!" moment that will illuminate the labyrinth of sociology.

Picture this: you're deeply involved in a group project, trying to convince your classmates to adopt your innovative idea of using quantum mechanics to address a social issue. As you enthusiastically explain how the uncertainty principle connects to human relationships, your sociology professor looks at you as if you suggested going camping in a black hole. Some of us made strong links between societal forces and their effects along with ideas from statistical mechanics and entropy (just to clarify, I wasn't the genius in this scenario, and I thought our group had a solid array of theoretical physics tools, but since I'm more focused on applied science—essentially engineering—I'll admit that). In that moment, you realize sociology isn't merely about finding the right answers; it's about understanding the questions that influence human behavior. It's like discovering that the key to your mom's famous cookie recipe isn't just the chocolate chips, but the understanding of why people have such a craving for cookies in the first place

As you explore the field of sociology, you may encounter ideas that connect with your analytical, STEM-oriented mindset. Consider sociology as an intricate experiment where the variables include human behavior, cultural norms, and social structures. In this context, you transform from merely analyzing data to becoming an inquisitive scientist investigating the unpredictable responses of other people. You might find yourself engaged in conversations about social stratification, recognizing that it resembles the process of organizing your data into defined categories. Who would have thought that grasping the social dynamics of your peers could be as exciting as calculating the path of a projectile? However, be warned: while we are naturally curious, the lack of rigorous demands after experiments can sometimes lead to a dislike for the field, especially in an introductory course where there is more flexibility. Additionally, some lecturers may come across as too confident to embrace new viewpoints.

Engagement strategies matter, especially when your professor begins to discuss the importance of community engagement while you're still trying to wrap your head around the idea that "social capital" has nothing to do with your bank account. Imagine if your sociology class was structured like a lab, with hands-on experiments where you could test hypotheses about social interactions. Instead of reading dry textbooks, you could be out in the field, conducting surveys on why your roommate insists on eating cereal with orange juice. This approach would not only keep your attention but might also lead to some insightful revelations about the quirks of human behavior – including, perhaps, your own.

Finally, let's talk about the faculty who teach these courses. Some professors have a knack for making sociology feel as engaging as a TED Talk while others may treat it like a dull lecture from the 1970s. If your sociology professor is more of a "sit down and let me bore you with statistics" type, you may find yourself daydreaming about your next engineering project. But when you encounter a professor who can weave sociology into a narrative as compelling as the latest Marvel movie, you'll find yourself having that "Eureka!" moment not just in the lab, but in the classroom too. You may leave the course not only with a better understanding of sociology but with a newfound appreciation for the chaotic, beautiful mess that is human society.

Chapter 3: Real-World Applications: Making Sociology Relevant for STEM Majors

The Sociology of Wi-Fi: A Study in Connectivity

In the brave new world of academia, where STEM students navigate a labyrinth of equations and algorithms, the mere mention of sociology often elicits groans louder than a Wi-Fi router rebooting after a power surge. Why? Because sociology, much like that one group project partner who insists on discussing their feelings instead of the assignment, brings a whole new dimension of complexity that many STEM majors didn't sign up for. Imagine trying to explain the intricate social fabric of human interaction while simultaneously calculating the trajectory of a rocket launch. It's like mixing oil and water, or worse, like trying to connect to Wi-Fi in a crowded coffee shop—everyone wants to, but nobody knows how.

As we delve into the sociology of Wi-Fi, let's consider how connectivity (or the lack thereof) mirrors social relationships. Picture this: you're in a lecture hall, the professor is waxing poetic about social networks, and you're just trying to connect to the campus Wi-Fi. The frustration builds as you realize that your connection is about as stable as your interest in the subject. Suddenly, you start wondering if the Wi-Fi signal strength is a metaphor for social capital. If only your social skills could buffer as quickly as your video stream during a Netflix binge. In this brave new world of digital sociology, Wi-Fi becomes a character in itself, representing our need for connection, both online and offline.

The real kicker, however, is how STEM students approach this labyrinth of connectivity. They're accustomed to clear parameters and definitive answers—only to be met with sociological theories that seem to have been designed by a committee of philosophers on a caffeine high. When faced with concepts like social stratification or collective consciousness, their heads may start spinning faster than their favorite CPU. It's like being asked to solve a Rubik's Cube while simultaneously explaining the nuances of Marxist theory. The struggle is real, and the groans can be heard echoing through the lecture halls like a haunting refrain.

To make sociology relevant for STEM majors, we must embrace the chaos of our digital lives. Wi-Fi isn't just about getting online; it's about understanding the networks we build, both virtual and physical. That Instagram feed? It's a sociological case study just waiting to be analyzed. Faculty need to harness this digital obsession, turning Wi-Fi metaphors into engaging lessons that illustrate the importance of social connections. Imagine a lecture where the professor compares Wi-Fi bandwidth to social influence—now that's a class worth attending. They could even throw in a few memes about connectivity woes to keep the students chuckling instead of groaning.

Finally, let's address the impact of faculty teaching styles on STEM student engagement. It's a delicate balance, akin to maintaining a stable internet connection during a thunderstorm. Professors who use jargon that sounds like it's been pulled straight from a sociology textbook can put STEM students to sleep faster than a malfunctioning projector. Instead, educators should channel their inner Wi-Fi router—

broadcasting knowledge with clarity and humor, while ensuring that everyone stays connected. By embracing a style that resonates with the tech-savvy minds of STEM students, faculty can transform sociology from a dreaded chore into an enlightening journey through the complex web of human interaction—one hilarious meme at a time.

When Algorithms Meet Humanity: Predicting Social Trends

When algorithms meet humanity, we find ourselves in a curious dance that looks suspiciously like a poorly choreographed flash mob. Imagine a group of STEM students, armed with their powerful calculators and algorithms, attempting to predict social trends as if they were plotting the trajectory of a rogue satellite. They eagerly input variables such as "number of coffee cups consumed" and "Twitter memes about cats" into their models, only to discover that human behavior is as unpredictable as the Wi-Fi signal at a crowded coffee shop. Spoiler alert: the results often lead to conclusions that are more baffling than enlightening.

STEM students, with their mathematical precision, often groan at the thought of sociology. Their brains are finely tuned to the predictable patterns of physics and chemistry, where the laws of nature are as reliable as their morning caffeine fix. Enter sociology, where the only law seems to be Murphy's Law: anything that can go wrong will go wrong, especially if you're trying to determine why people suddenly start wearing socks with sandals. The irony is thick as students realize that the same algorithms they use to predict the trajectory of a projectile can't quite nail down why their roommate binge-watched a reality show about competitive cheese rolling.

Learning styles play an amusing role in the intersection of STEM and sociology. While STEM students thrive on empirical data and concrete answers, sociology seems to revel in the gray areas of human emotion and social constructs. Picture a group of students trying to apply their beloved scientific method to a sociology class discussion about the societal implications of avocado toast. The ensuing debate could rival a soap opera, complete with dramatic pauses and impassioned pleas to "consider the cultural significance!" It's a classic case of engineers attempting to build a bridge over a swamp, only to find themselves knee-deep in the quagmire of subjective interpretations.

As STEM majors grapple with sociology's unique vernacular, the language barrier becomes a source of unintentional comedy. Terms like "social capital" and "cultural hegemony" sound like Buzzfeed quizzes gone wrong. Imagine a STEM student earnestly asking for a PowerPoint presentation on "how to calculate cultural hegemony," only to receive a lecture that feels more like a TED Talk on the ethics of avocado consumption. The confusion leads to a delightful moment when they realize their algorithms don't apply to the whims of social trends, and they are left contemplating the deeper meaning of why people really prefer memes over meaningful discourse.

Engagement strategies in sociology classes often resemble a game of charades, with professors armed with colorful graphs and anecdotes, while students' eyes glaze over at the thought of yet another group project. Picture a professor enthusiastically describing the impact of social media on modern relationships, while the STEM students covertly calculate the probability of an actual connection happening in a world dominated by emojis. The impact of faculty teaching styles becomes evident as some professors manage to weave humor and relatability into their lectures, making even the most complex theories seem like a fun game of trivia. Others, however, resemble mad scientists, leaving students to wonder if they'll ever escape the labyrinth of social theory and return to the comforting arms of predictable equations.

The Physics of Social Media: It's All Just Gravity

When we think about gravity, we picture apples falling from trees and our own unfortunate attempts to lift weights. But let's pivot to social media, the invisible force pulling us into endless scrolling and cat videos. In the grand scheme of things, social media operates like gravity: it's all about attraction, repulsion, and the occasional collision with reality. Just like the laws of physics govern celestial bodies, social media algorithms dictate what we see and, more importantly, what we can't escape. STEM students, with their penchant for logic, might find it hard to grasp that the same principles of attraction that keep planets in orbit also keep us glued to our screens.

Consider the way social media platforms act like cosmic black holes, sucking in everything with their gravitational pull. You start with a harmless scroll through your friend's vacation photos, and before you know it, you've traversed into the deep space of conspiracy theories about lizard people. Just as gravity bends light, social media bends our perception of reality, distorting the truth into something more palatable—or, more likely, more outrageous. The heavy influence of likes, shares, and comments creates a force field that can warp even the most rational STEM minds into believing that their neighbor's avocado toast is, in fact, an acceptable form of culinary genius.

Now, let's talk about the engagement strategies that keep STEM students interested in this chaotic universe. What if sociology were presented with the same excitement as a lab experiment? Imagine a sociology class where students could conduct a social media experiment: tracking how many likes a picture of a potato gets compared to a picture of a puppy. They'd be measuring the gravitational pull of cuteness versus starchiness, and who wouldn't be fascinated by that? Instead of memorizing definitions, they'd be collecting data and hypothesizing why their potato post flopped. After all, if gravity can keep planets in line, surely a little fun can keep STEM students awake and engaged.

But here's the kicker: the language barrier. For STEM students, sociology often feels like it was written in a different gravitational field. Terms like "social capital" and "cultural hegemony" might as well be alien physics equations. They sit in class, hoping for a light-speed translation of these concepts into something they can relate to—maybe something like, "Social media is like a chemical reaction, where the right mixture of influencers can create explosive engagement." If only professors could incorporate a few equations or graphs, perhaps the enlightenment would strike like a bolt of lightning, breaking through the dark clouds of confusion.

As we navigate this cosmic interplay between gravity and social media, let's not forget the impact of faculty teaching styles. Picture a professor who approaches sociology with the same fervor as a physics lecturer explaining gravity's role in space travel. Suddenly, the classroom transforms into a launchpad for ideas, where discussions about social media trends become as thrilling as rocket science. When faculty can blend humor with the complexities of sociology, STEM students might just realize that understanding social interactions isn't so far from understanding the laws of motion. After all, whether we're discussing Newton's laws or the latest TikTok trend, the forces at play are all around us, and they're just waiting to be explored—with a touch of laughter along the way.

However, it is effective. (Toy models utilizing mathematics provide better predictions of trends!?)

It truly works. Mathematical toy models provide remarkably improved predictions for trends! Who would have ever imagined that a series of equations hastily jotted down on a whiteboard could unlock the intricate secrets of human behavior? Picture a dedicated group of STEM students, calculators in hand, diligently inputting various social variables like 'awkward first dates' and 'overcooked spaghetti.' They might find themselves perplexed and bewildered by the fact that people often do not adhere to a simple linear regression model when it comes to matters of love or culinary mishaps. However, if you can employ calculus to determine how quickly your coffee cools down, then surely you can navigate the complexities and nuances of human interactions—right?

Let's face it, we're all a little skeptical when it comes to sociology. It's like that charming but unreliable friend who always has a wild story to share but never seems to have any solid evidence to back it up. "Oh, sure, people behave differently in groups," we nod along, while secretly calculating the odds of them getting it wrong this time. But then, when those toy models—yes, the ones that look like they belong in a preschool classroom—start churning out predictions that actually make sense and align with reality, we can't help but raise an eyebrow in surprise. Suddenly, the "social scientists" aren't just talking about feelings and abstract concepts; they're crunching numbers and using data to tell us when the next viral TikTok dance will take over social media and capture everyone's attention.

Picture the thrill in the classroom when the sociology professor reveals a new project involving toy models. The STEM students sit up, half-expecting to create some complex invention that could transform social theory. Instead, they find themselves with a box of Legos, tasked to construct a representation of social networks. Cue the collective sigh of disappointment. Yet, as they begin stacking the bricks, they discover an unexpected joy in visualizing social interactions through these vibrant plastic pieces. Who would have thought that a simple model could shed light on why their group projects always spiral into chaos? Spoiler alert: it might just be the therapeutic nature of playing with Legos that truly benefits us, much like the stereotypes about our schedules actually hold some truth amid the relentless cycle of assignments, reports, labs, and more (p.s. I think you all can relate to this)

Yet, the real magic unfolds when these models begin to reflect real-world trends in a striking manner. Suddenly, the STEM students are no longer just passively listening to lectures about social behavior; instead, they're actively engaging with data that truly resonates with them on a deeper level. They start to recognize intriguing correlations between their carefully crafted models and the actual social phenomena that are occurring around them in their everyday lives. "Wait a minute," one student exclaims, a mix of surprise and realization lighting up their face, "are you telling me that my math skills can actually help me understand why nobody seems willing to work with me on group assignments?" This lightbulb moment is not just illuminating; it's downright hilarious, as they come to terms with the complex social dynamics at play in their academic lives. The revelation spreads through the group, and suddenly a bunch of us find ourselves becoming the next generation of "economists", crunching data to explain away our social challenges. It is

31

genuinely fun to engage in this analytical process once in a while, but when we delve into the data and uncover the root causes of our social interactions, it can sometimes lead to valuable insights that genuinely enhance our social lives.

By the end of the course, our once-skeptical STEM students have become unlikely fans of sociology, all thanks to their toy models. They've learned that while people may not always follow the rules of mathematics, the patterns that emerge can offer surprising insights. They leave the class with a newfound appreciation for the messy, unpredictable nature of human behavior, and perhaps a sense of camaraderie with their sociological counterparts. Who knew that a little playful modeling could bridge the vast chasm between STEM and sociology? In the grand scheme of things, if you can predict trends with a few toy figures and some equations, maybe—just maybe—sociology isn't that bad after all.

Chapter 4: The Language Barrier: Terminology Differences Between STEM and Sociology

"Social Constructs": Not a New Type of Engineering

In the land of academia, there are two tribes that often clash in ways that make a "Game of Thrones" battle look like a polite dinner party: STEM (science, technology, engineering, and mathematics) and sociology. While STEM scholars are busy building bridges, rockets, and algorithms, sociologists are in their cozy corner discussing, well, how those bridges, rockets, and algorithms are socially constructed. And if you thought "construct" was a word with a fixed meaning, brace yourself—because in sociology, it's like the concept of a "puzzle piece" that refuses to fit into the logical picture.

Take the term "social construct" for example. In sociology, "social construct" is like their all-knowing god of theory. Race, gender, class—yep, they're all "social constructs" that exist solely because humans collectively agreed they should. Sociologists love to point out that these constructs don't exist in the physical world (like, say, atoms or bridges), but rather in the metaphysical, constantly shifting, ever-evolving "realm of human thought." Imagine trying to apply that to your next engineering project: "I'm not sure what went wrong with the bridge, but maybe it's just a social construct!"

In case you're wondering, this isn't some new type of engineering—sociologists aren't going around designing socially constructed bridges that fall over every time a strong opinion is voiced about gender. Instead, what they're really talking about is how concepts like race, gender, or class have no inherent physical basis but are instead defined by society. So while engineers are busy ensuring structural integrity, sociologists are making sure that those same structures don't accidentally reinforce outdated norms. Good luck applying that to your next blueprint.

In the engineering world, "construct" means something completely different—namely, it's a thing that exists, can be measured, and most importantly, doesn't make people's heads spin when you talk about it. A bridge is a construct. A building is a construct. You can measure them, observe them, and even test them to ensure they don't collapse under the weight of too many people who disagree with each other. But the term "social construct" in sociology doesn't fit in this neat, physical framework. In fact, it's the academic equivalent of deciding that a chair doesn't exist because it's socially constructed to be something you sit in, rather than a metaphor for a power dynamic in society.

Sociologists would say, "Oh, but race is a social construct. We made it up!" To which an engineer might respond, "Okay, so, um, does that mean I can just build a bridge that doesn't have to follow the laws of physics? Because that's a construct too, right?" Sociologists would probably reply, "You're misunderstanding me. It's the perception of the bridge's stability that's constructed." And the engineer, after checking to see if they've slipped into an alternate dimension where logic has been outlawed, would slowly back away.

Here's the thing: engineers and scientists love constructs because they're predictable. They adhere to rules.

They follow principles. They are built on empirical evidence. Social constructs? Well, they're not exactly what you'd call reliable. You can't measure them with a ruler, and no matter how hard you try, you can't test them for strength or load-bearing capacity in a controlled lab environment. But sociologists will still argue that constructs like race or gender do have real-world impacts, even if they don't fit neatly into a testable framework. Because, you know, it's all about social interactions and historical contexts. So, while engineers are out here building physical structures, sociologists are building their theories and then asking everyone to just believe that their constructs are just as, if not more, important.

If you wanted to understand this difference from a sociological point of view, you might hear: "Race isn't a biological concept, it's a social one." Engineers, on the other hand, might just say, "Okay, so if I wanted to build a bridge using social constructs, do I just ask people to imagine it in their minds until it's done?"

When you bring the term "social construct" into a conversation about STEM, things get messy. Take a simple engineering question: "How do we build a more sustainable city?" An engineer might point to technological advances like solar panels, green building materials, or efficient transportation systems. A sociologist might ask, "But have you considered how urban spaces are socially constructed?" Translation: "Did you consider how the people in the city interact with those solar panels and whether or not those buildings reinforce power structures?"

You can almost hear the engineer's brain grinding to a halt. What do power structures have to do with solar panels? But that's exactly the beauty of the sociological construct— nothing is ever quite what it seems. Those "solar panels" might represent the effort to reduce inequality, or they might reinforce the gap between rich and poor, depending on who gets access to them. And therein lies the complexity. Sociologists often deliberately avoid any empirical measurement because they're more interested in the nuances of human behavior and how those behaviors shape societal systems. The problem is, engineers like to measure things in inches, volts, and decimals. Sociologists? Well, they measure society with words and concepts that never quite seem to fit in a 3D model.

It's not that sociology has nothing valuable to offer; in fact, it provides insights that can greatly improve engineering and technology, especially in fields like ethics, social justice, and human-centered design. However, the language barrier between STEM and sociology is real. Engineers use precise, quantifiable terminology, while sociologists throw around terms like "social construct" that sound, frankly, like they belong in a philosophy class rather than a construction meeting.

For example, engineers working on technology for marginalized communities would need to understand concepts like social constructs to design equitable solutions. But don't expect them to suddenly become fluent in sociology. It's like asking a sociologist to build a bridge and expect them to pass the structural integrity tests. It's just not going to happen.

So, let's accept that social constructs aren't "just another type of engineering," and maybe give sociology credit for tackling issues that engineers never thought to address in the first place—like, say, the socio-political forces that dictate where the bridges get built.

The Great Debate: Theory vs. Hypothesis

In the grand arena of academia, where theories clash like titans and hypotheses scuttle around like over-caffeinated crabs, we find ourselves at the heart of a great debate: Theory vs. Hypothesis. For the average STEM student, this battle resembles a chaotic game of dodgeball, where the rules are unclear, the players are confused, and everyone is just trying not to get hit in the face by a rogue idea. Theories, those grandiose constructs built on the backs of countless experiments and peer-reviewed papers, stand tall like the imposing structures of a university campus. In contrast, hypotheses are the scrappy underdogs, those bold predictions that emerge from the murky depths of curiosity, often inspired by a late-night study session fueled by pizza and existential dread.

STEM students, with their penchant for equations and algorithms, often approach sociology with the same enthusiasm as a cat confronting a cucumber. The very notion of diving into the murky waters of social theories can be daunting. Why bother with a theory that can't be measured with a precise formula? Why think about the nuances of societal constructs when you could be calculating the trajectory of a projectile? This philosophical wrestling match leaves many STEM students groaning at the thought of dragging themselves through Sociology 101, where the playful banter of theorists feels more like a Shakespearean drama than a straightforward scientific inquiry.

Engagement strategies, dear reader, often resemble the frantic attempts of a parent trying to get their child to eat broccoli. Professors might try to relate sociological theories to the STEM students' world by likening a social structure to a complex algorithm. "Just think of society as a massive network of interconnected nodes!" they might proclaim, while the students silently wonder if they can just program a simulation of a society instead. The challenge lies not only in bridging the gap between the two fields but in making sociology feel as exciting as the latest tech gadget or scientific breakthrough. After all, who wouldn't prefer discussing the latest advancements in artificial intelligence over the intricacies of social stratification?

Then we encounter the language barrier, where terminology differences become a comedic skit waiting to happen. For STEM majors, the term "social construct" might as well refer to a poorly built robot. Meanwhile, sociologists toss around phrases like "cultural hegemony" and "symbolic interactionism" as if they're discussing the weather. This leads to a delightful scene in the classroom, where STEM students nod along, trying to decipher the sociological code while mentally calculating how many lab hours they'll lose by attending this class. The hope is that one day, a brave soul will create a bilingual glossary to translate between the two worlds, saving countless hours of confusion and perhaps a few sanity points.

Ultimately, the impact of faculty teaching styles plays a pivotal role in this comedy of errors. Some professors, with the enthusiasm of a game show host, attempt to draw connections between abstract sociological theories and the concrete realities of STEM fields. Others, however, may come across as those overly serious scientists who refuse to crack a smile, leaving students to wonder if they've accidentally walked into a funeral instead of a lecture. The key to winning the hearts of STEM students lies in humor, relatable examples, and the occasional meme that could lighten the mood and spark interest. After all, who could resist a well-timed joke about social stratification that also references the latest breakthrough in quantum computing? In this great debate, laughter may just be the bridge that connects two seemingly disparate worlds.

Where is your data?: interpretations over facts

In the grand quest for knowledge, STEM students often find themselves trapped in the bewildering labyrinth of sociology, a field that sometimes feels like it was constructed by a committee of philosophers on a caffeine high. One of the most delightful, yet perplexing, aspects of sociology is the phrase "Where is your data?" which is often uttered by professors as if they are summoning a genie from a bottle. For STEM students, accustomed to the concrete certainty of numbers and equations, this question can feel like being asked to locate the Holy Grail in a sea of interpretive dance performances.

Imagine a STEM student, freshly liberated from the rigid confines of equations and graphs, entering a sociology lecture only to be bombarded with terms like "social construct" and "cultural relativism." It's as if they've walked into a room where everyone is playing charades while simultaneously discussing the existential crisis of a toaster. So when the professor poses the query about data, the STEM student glances around, hoping someone has a PowerPoint slide with a pie chart to back up the abstract concepts being thrown around. Unfortunately, all they find are more questions, and maybe a few stray cats that wandered in during the discussion.

The irony is that in sociology, data is often less about hard numbers and more about interpretations that can make a room full of students groan in unison. To a STEM student, who thrives on quantifiable evidence, this is akin to asking a mathematician to solve a problem using only interpretive dance. The varying interpretations of sociological concepts can lead to some eyebrow-raising conclusions, such as determining the societal impact of cat memes, which, in the world of STEM, would likely be dismissed as frivolous. Yet, here we are, grappling with the idea that the emotional resonance of a cat meme can hold more weight than the findings of a well-structured experiment.

Yet, let's not dismiss sociology entirely as a whimsical distraction. It has real-world applications that can enhance a STEM student's understanding of human behavior. After all, who can design a better app than someone who understands the emotional nuances of their users? However, the challenge remains: how do we bridge the seemingly insurmountable gap between the hard facts of STEM and the soft, squishy interpretations of sociology? Perhaps a blend of statistics and heartfelt storytelling is the answer, allowing STEM students to see how data can tell a story and engage them in discussions that don't require a thesaurus to decipher.

In conclusion, the next time a sociology professor asks, "Where is your data?", remember that it's not just a question; it's an invitation to explore the wild world of interpretations. Embrace the chaos, and let it remind you that while STEM provides the tools to dissect the universe, sociology offers the map to navigate the human experience. So, let's raise a toast to the brave STEM souls who dare to tread into sociology, armed with their calculators and a sense of humor, ready to decipher the mysteries of society, one groan at a time.

Jargon Jousting: Who Can Speak the Weirdest Language?

In the grand arena of academia, where the noble warriors of STEM clash with the enigmatic scholars of sociology, a curious phenomenon arises: jargon jousting. Picture this: a STEM student, fresh from deciphering the latest algorithm, suddenly finds themselves in a sociology lecture filled with terms like "hegemonic masculinity" and "social stratification." It's as if they've entered a different dimension where the laws of language are rewritten, and every word feels like a medieval weapon designed to confuse and bewilder. It's a linguistic duel, and the stakes are high—most notably, the GPA.

STEM students, with their precision and logic, often approach sociology with the same mindset they use to tackle differential equations. They expect clear definitions and straightforward applications. Instead, they are met with a barrage of phrases that sound like they were plucked from a particularly pretentious poetry slam. "Cultural hegemony?" What is that, a fancy way of saying "everyone thinks the same"? And don't even get them started on "intersectionality." To a budding engineer, that might sound like a new type of bridge design, not a complex web of social identities. The bewilderment is real, and the groans can be heard echoing through lecture halls.

Now, let's not forget the sociology majors, who wield their jargon like knights brandishing swords, ready to defend their territory from the onslaught of STEM logic. They toss around terms like "postmodernism" and "quantitative research" as if they're discussing the weather, while STEM students are left wondering if they need a translator. The sociologists might as well be speaking Elvish, while STEM students are frantically Googling terms under their desks. It's a classic case of "Who can make the other group feel more bewildered?" Spoiler alert: it's usually the sociology majors, who thrive in this linguistic chaos.

Engagement strategies in this context become a battle of wits and whimsy. Professors must don their armor—metaphorically speaking, of course—and find ways to bridge this chasm of jargon. Perhaps they could introduce a game called "Jargon Joust," where students earn points for translating complex terms into plain English. The winner gets a shiny trophy, perhaps a golden calculator, and the satisfaction of knowing they survived the linguistic labyrinth. Or they could hold a "Sociology for Engineers" night, complete with snacks and a glossary of terms, so STEM students can feel less like they're wandering through a dark forest of confusing concepts.

Ultimately, the goal is to foster a dialogue that allows both sides to learn, laugh, and embrace the absurdity of it all. If STEM students can survive the onslaught of sociological jargon, they might even discover that beneath the layers of confusing language lies a fascinating realm of social dynamics that can enrich their understanding of the world. And if nothing else, they'll leave with a newfound appreciation for the power of language—whether it's the precise language of STEM or the whimsical, often perplexing dialect of sociology. In the end, it's all just a game of words, and everyone deserves a chance to play.

Chapter 5: Engagement Strategies: Keeping STEM Students Interested in Sociology

Gamifying Sociology: Who Wants to Play "Sociological Survivor"?

In the grand arena of academia, where the gladiators of STEM clash with the philosophers of sociology, emerges a revolutionary game: "Sociological Survivor." Picture this: STEM students, armed with calculators and a healthy dose of skepticism, pitted against the social sciences in a battle for knowledge supremacy. The rules are simple: survive the semester by dodging theoretical jargon, deciphering the language of social constructs, and forming alliances with your sociology professor while maintaining your sanity. In this game, the only true measure of success is whether you can make it through a lecture without asking, "But how does this relate to my coding project?"

As the game unfolds, contestants must navigate through the treacherous waters of sociology terminology, which can feel like a foreign language designed specifically to confuse. Think of it as a scavenger hunt but instead of finding hidden treasures, you're frantically searching for the meaning of "hegemonic masculinity" or "structural functionalism" while your classmates throw around terms like "social capital" as if they're discussing the latest iPhone features. Every time someone mentions "intersectionality," you can almost hear the collective groan of STEM students trying to intersect their clear-cut equations with the murky world of societal dynamics.

Bonus points if you can decode the meanings without Googling them mid-class!

The challenges don't stop there; surviving sociology requires strategic alliances. Forming a study group is essential, where STEM students can join forces against the onslaught of social theories. Picture a group of future engineers huddled in a corner, attempting to apply the laws of physics to justify their existence in a class discussing the impact of social structures. The laughter that ensues when someone proposes to create a flowchart of "the socialization process" is a testament to the absurdity of trying to apply rigid logic to the beautiful chaos of human interaction. In this game, humor becomes the ultimate survival tool.

As the semester drags on, the stakes get higher. Faculty teaching styles can either make or break your chances of survival. Some professors adopt a "Survivor: Sociology Edition" approach, throwing pop quizzes like immunity challenges, while others prefer the serene "let's sit around the campfire and discuss our feelings" style. For STEM students, who are accustomed to clear guidelines and structured labs, the unpredictability of a sociology class can feel like a surprise elimination round. The key to thriving lies in mastering the art of engagement strategies—like feigning interest in the group project on "The Role of Media in Society" while secretly calculating how many hours you can devote to it without sacrificing your GPA.

Ultimately, by the end of the semester, you'll either emerge as the reigning champion of "Sociological Survivor" or stumble out with a newfound appreciation for the social sciences—albeit one that you're still struggling to articulate without using a flowchart. Whether you've mastered the language of sociology or you're still hiding behind your

STEM credentials, remember that every great survivor has a story to tell. So, grab your metaphorical torch, and let's navigate this wild, unpredictable terrain together. After all, it's all in the name of survival, and maybe—just maybe—you'll laugh through the pain.

Using Excel to Analyze Feelings: A STEM Student's Dream

Imagine a world where feelings are as quantifiable as the pH levels in your lab samples. For STEM students, the idea of analyzing emotions might sound like a cruel joke, but fear not—Excel is here to rescue you from the abyss of sociological despair. Picture this: you can input your emotional data into a spreadsheet, and with a few clicks, you can create graphs that illustrate your existential dread. After all, nothing says "I'm coping" quite like a pie chart showing the percentage of your anxiety over midterms versus your fear of group projects in sociology class.

The first step in this emotional analysis journey is to collect your feelings. Sure, you might not have the time to sit down and meditate on your emotions (you have a robotics project due and a lab report that's mocking you), but you can at least start documenting your mood swings in Excel. Create a simple spreadsheet with columns labeled "Date," "Feeling," and "Reason." As a STEM student, you know that data collection is key, so don't shy away from logging every instance of frustration—whether it's from a particularly dense reading or your professor's insistence on using "qualitative" instead of "this makes no sense."

Next, once you've accumulated enough data, it's time to dive into the world of formulas. You can calculate the average number of times you've felt overwhelmed per week, or even better, create a regression model predicting when you'll next break down during a lecture. Picture the satisfaction of presenting your findings to classmates: "According to my linear regression analysis, my chances of crying in sociology class increase by 25% every time I hear the word 'paradigm.'" Your peers will either be impressed or concerned, but either way, you'll have succeeded in making the subject matter a little more relatable.

Now, let's discuss visualization. Excel offers a plethora of chart options, and you can use them to showcase your emotional rollercoaster. A line graph can effectively illustrate the sharp peaks of despair during exam season, while a bar graph can highlight the emotional toll of group projects compared to solo assignments. Just remember to add a legend—because what good is a chart if your classmates don't know that the red spikes correspond to your "I wish I had chosen a different major" moments?

Finally, after you've created your emotional data visualizations, it's time to present them. Don't be surprised if your classmates are more engaged by your Excel charts than by the actual content of the course. You'll have successfully turned your feelings into a form of art that even the most apathetic sociology major can appreciate. Who knew that combining STEM skills with emotional data could lead to laughs, camaraderie, and maybe even a group therapy session masquerading as a study group? Excel has transformed your emotional struggles into a STEM student's dream, proving once again that laughter is indeed the best reaction to the chaos of college life.

Reality TV as a Case Study: Sociology or Just Drama?

Reality TV serves as a fascinating case study in the intersection of sociology and drama, particularly for STEM students who often view sociology through a lens of bemused detachment. Picture this: a bunch of people stranded on an island, competing for food and fame, while the rest of us are safely nestled in our cozy dorm rooms, snickering at their misadventures. As STEM students, we're used to equations and experiments, not emotional breakdowns over who stole the last slice of pizza. Yet, here we are, witnessing what sociologists might describe as a "microcosm of society." Meanwhile, we're just trying to figure out how to calculate the probability of someone crying over a rose.

When we dive into the sociology of reality TV, it's like watching a slow-motion train wreck—compelling, but also slightly horrifying. These shows present us with a parade of behaviors that are ripe for analysis. From alliances formed in the heat of competition to the inevitable backstabbing, it's a social experiment gone awry. One might argue that the producers are performing a social experiment for us, but let's be real: they're just looking for the most outrageous content to keep ratings high. For STEM majors, this raises a critical question: is this really sociology, or just glorified drama? Spoiler alert: it's both, with a generous sprinkling of ridiculousness.

The language barrier is where things get entertaining. Sociology has its own lexicon that often sounds like it was written during a caffeine-fueled late-night study session. Terms like "social stratification" and "symbolic interactionism" can feel as foreign as advanced calculus to a sociology major. Meanwhile, reality TV participants are busy throwing around phrases like "totally betrayed" and "game-changer." If only we could merge these worlds! Imagine a reality show where contestants explained their emotional turmoil through the lens of sociological theories. "I felt a strong sense of anomie when my alliance crumbled," could easily replace "I was heartbroken when they voted me off the island."

Engagement strategies for STEM students often involve humor and relatability. Reality TV unwittingly provides a treasure trove of sociological concepts wrapped in drama. Faculty members could leverage this by assigning episodes as case studies. Instead of dry readings, students could analyze the social dynamics at play while munching popcorn. Picture a classroom full of STEM students passionately debating the implications of a contestant's social strategy, using terms like "functionalism" and "deviance" in the same breath as "betrayal" and "dramatic exit." Suddenly, sociology doesn't seem so dull, and students find themselves invested in the social experiment—no calculus required.

Ultimately, the impact of faculty teaching styles cannot be overlooked. A professor who can weave the absurdity of reality TV into their lectures will likely have a more engaged classroom. If they can elicit laughter while explaining the complexities of social interaction, then they've struck gold. After all, who wouldn't want to discuss the sociological implications of a contestant's emotional breakdown over a token? By embracing the drama of reality TV, educators can turn what was once groan-worthy into a lively discussion about the human experience, all while STEM students secretly hope for a surprise twist ending.

Give me the equation....please, I'm begging you.

In the grand theater of academia, where equations dance with the elegance of a prima ballerina and theories pirouette gracefully across the stage, sociology steps in like an awkward uncle at a family gathering. "Give me the equation... please, I'm begging you," is the silent prayer of every STEM student as they sit squirming in a Sociology 101 lecture. The only thing we're accustomed to is the comforting embrace of numbers, symbols, and the occasional Greek letter that feels like an old friend. Instead, we find ourselves grappling with concepts like social stratification and cultural hegemony, which sound suspiciously like fancy names for that one cousin who always brings the weird dip to family parties.

As we flip through the pages of our sociology textbooks, we often find ourselves wondering how we got here. STEM majors are trained to dissect the world through equations, models, and experiments. The only "social dynamics" we're interested in involve the velocity of a car or the trajectory of a projectile. The shift from the precise world of calculus to the nebulous realm of sociology feels like being asked to trade in our well-oiled scientific calculators for a crystal ball. Yet, here we are, forced to untangle the complexities of human behavior without any quantitative data to anchor our thoughts. It's like trying to build a bridge made of spaghetti—fascinating, but not exactly sturdy.

In our quest for relevance, we STEM students often look for the proverbial equation that can sum up the social phenomena we encounter. We want a neat formula that can reduce the complexities of human interaction into a single line: "Social Behavior = X + Y + Z." Alas, sociology offers us a buffet of variables with no clear relationship, leaving us hungry for something that feels more substantial. Our minds crave the predictable patterns of scientific inquiry, but sociology insists on throwing in the wild card of human emotion. If only we could derive a function that explains why our classmates seem to have endless energy for discussing "theories of the self" while we desperately clutch our coffee mugs, yearning for a good old-fashioned lab experiment.

The language barrier adds another layer of complexity to our sociological plight. Where we see "variables," sociologists see "social constructs." It's like trying to decipher a foreign language where the vocabulary is rooted in philosophy and the grammar is based on feelings. We're left feeling like we missed the memo on the latest slang while our sociology peers chatter away with fervor, throwing around terms like "intersectionality" and "cultural relativism" as if they're the latest trends in fashion. Meanwhile, all we can think about is how to model the perfect graph, wishing that at least one concept would lend itself to a good ol' fashioned pie chart.

In the end, what keeps us engaged in this sociological circus is the realization that even though we might groan about it, there's a certain charm to the chaos. The impact of faculty teaching styles can't be underestimated; a professor who can weave humor into their lectures or relate sociological concepts to our beloved STEM fields can make all the difference. Perhaps we can find a way to connect the dots between our structured world of formulas and the unpredictable nature of human society. So here we sit, oscillating between groans and guffaws, trying to make sense of the madness. As we cling to our calculators with one hand, let's embrace the ridiculousness of it all, hoping that somewhere in this journey, we might just find the equation that makes sociology resonate with our STEM hearts.

Chapter 6: The Impact of Faculty Teaching Styles on STEM Student Engagement

The Lecture: A One-Way Ticket to Snoozeville

The lecture hall is often viewed as the Bermuda Triangle for STEM students: once inside, they lose all sense of time, engagement, and, quite frankly, will to live. The instructor stands at the front, armed with a PowerPoint presentation that rivals the length of War and Peace. As the lights dim and the projector hums to life, you can almost hear the collective groan of students who know they've been handed a one-way ticket to Snoozeville. While the professor passionately discusses the intricacies of social stratification, the STEM students are left wondering if they should have just stayed home and perfected their latest algorithm instead.

For STEM students, learning is often a hands-on experience, filled with experiments, labs, and coding marathons. So, when faced with a lecture that feels akin to watching paint dry, it's no surprise that their minds wander into the realm of daydreams where they're busy solving complex equations or contemplating the existence of a parallel universe where sociology doesn't exist. As the instructor drones on about social theory, students are mentally drafting their next engineering project or plotting how to escape the lecture without it being obvious. The reality is that most STEM students have a learning style that thrives on interaction, not passive absorption of information delivered at the speed of molasses.

Yet, there lies a silver lining in this storm cloud of boredom. If sociology could somehow be linked to actual applications that resonate with STEM majors, perhaps the lecture could transform from a snooze fest into an enlightening experience. Imagine a course where discussions about social networks are paired with the latest developments in machine learning, or where issues of inequality are interwoven with data analysis. If only someone could bridge that gap, transforming the lecture into a thrilling chase of knowledge instead of a leisurely stroll through the land of monotony.

Language, too, plays a pivotal role in this comedy of errors. The lexicon of sociology often feels like it was crafted in a different universe. Terms like "hegemonic power" and "cultural capital" might as well be written in hieroglyphics for the average STEM student. Meanwhile, professors enthusiastically toss around jargon like confetti at a parade, blissfully unaware of the glazed expressions staring back at them. The need for a translator becomes evident, as students struggle to decode the meaning behind the terms while simultaneously trying to stay awake. If only someone would introduce a "Sociology for Dummies" guide, perhaps lectures would become less of a linguistic labyrinth and more of a straightforward path to understanding.

Finally, the impact of faculty teaching styles cannot be overlooked in this quest for engagement. Some professors seem to think that simply reading from a script will ignite the flames of passion for sociology in their STEM students. Spoiler alert: it doesn't. The best professors are those who inject personality into their lectures, sprinkle in some humor, and encourage discussion. They understand that STEM students thrive on interaction and appreciate a good laugh, even when discussing the most serious of topics. When faculty members embrace innovative teaching strategies—like incorporating interactive discussions, real-world case studies, and even the occasional meme—students are far more likely to stay awake, engaged, and maybe even enjoy the ride through the world of sociology.

Professors Who Think They're Stand-Up Comedians

In the grand theater of academia, where the audience is often more interested in their smartphones than the lecture, some professors bravely take the stage with a delusional confidence that rivals the best stand-up comedians. They stride into the classroom, armed not with a syllabus, but with a collection of one-liners and a penchant for puns. These professors believe that their comedic interventions will transform the dreaded Sociology 101 into a laugh-a-minute extravaganza. Unfortunately, while they may envision themselves as the next big comedy sensation, what they often deliver is more akin to a cringe-inducing open mic night at a local coffee shop, where even the barista has left the premises.

As STEM students, we enter these lectures with the hope of unraveling the complex threads of human behavior and social structures, only to find ourselves trapped in a web of dad jokes and awkward pauses. Imagine sitting in a class where the professor starts with, "Why did the sociologist bring a ladder to class? To reach new heights of understanding!" Cue the groans, the eye rolls, and the collective questioning of life choices. These professors may not realize that while humor can be a bridge to engagement, their attempts often result in a chasm of confusion, leaving us to wonder if we accidentally signed up for a comedy workshop instead of an enlightening course.

The challenge escalates when these jokesters attempt to weave humor into sociological concepts that could use a little less levity and a bit more clarity. One moment, they're delivering a punchline about social stratification, and the next, they're expecting us to understand the intricacies of Marxist theory through a series of poorly timed quips. For the STEM student, who thrives on precision and logical reasoning, this is akin to trying to solve a mathematical equation while someone is constantly yelling jokes in the background. We find ourselves caught in a paradox: wanting to appreciate the humor but simultaneously yearning for a straightforward explanation of the material.

Engagement strategies, in theory, should enhance our understanding, yet when humor becomes the central focus, we often leave the lecture more entertained than educated. The professors who think they're comedians sometimes create an environment where learning resembles a game show, complete with awkward audience participation and laughter that feels more obligatory than genuine. As we navigate this comedic landscape, we can't help but wonder if these professors are more invested in their stand-up routine than in our scholarly success. The once-promising conversation about social issues becomes a series of punchlines that leave us more perplexed than enlightened.

Ultimately, while we appreciate the effort to make Sociology 101 bearable, we find ourselves longing for a balance between humor and substance. A sprinkle of levity can indeed lighten the mood, but when the punchline overshadows the point, we risk missing the critical lessons that sociology has to offer. In the end, we'd rather not have to decipher the hidden meanings behind a poorly delivered joke. Instead, we crave the straightforward, insightful discussions that make the complexities of human society not only relatable but also relevant to our lives as STEM students. After all, laughter is great, but understanding the world around us is even better.

Professors Who Think They're Scientists

In the grand theater of academia, there exists a unique breed of professor who struts around the sociology department as if they've just returned from a groundbreaking expedition in the lab. These are the "Professors Who Think They're Scientists," convinced that the study of human behavior is just a series of hypotheses waiting to be tested under the harsh glare of a microscope. You can spot them easily: they're the ones donning lab coats over their tweed jackets, clutching a clipboard as if it contains the secrets to the universe, all while trying to connect the dots between Karl Marx and quantum physics. Spoiler alert: they can't, and you'll be lucky if you make it through a lecture without hearing about their "innovative" method of analyzing social phenomena through the lens of statistical significance.

Every sociology 101 class has its fair share of these well-intentioned professors who approach the subject with the same enthusiasm they would reserve for a groundbreaking scientific discovery. They believe that their background in the hard sciences lends them an air of credibility in the social sciences, which is about as accurate as using a rubber chicken as a model for a biological organism. Students sit in the back, rolling their eyes as their professors launch into elaborate explanations of social dynamics that sound suspiciously like poorly interpreted data sets. It's a rare skill to manage to make discussions about societal norms feel as dry as a lab report, but somehow, these professors excel at it.

As STEM students, we come into sociology class equipped with our calculators, equations, and a healthy dose of skepticism. We're trained to seek out tangible results, rigorously test our ideas, and validate our findings with numbers. Imagine our horror when confronted with a professor who insists that the outcome of a study on group behavior is just as scientifically valid as our latest experiment on the tensile strength of materials. You can practically hear the collective groan as we realize we're expected to engage with a subject that relies heavily on subjective interpretations rather than hard data. It's like asking a physicist to critique a Shakespearean sonnet—there's a disconnect that no amount of sociological theory can bridge.

Engagement strategies become a Herculean task when you're dealing with these self-proclaimed social scientists. They often attempt to spark interest through bizarre experiments that would make even the most adventurous STEM student cringe. Picture this: a classroom filled with students trying to understand group dynamics by forming a human chain while the professor meticulously records their "data" on a whiteboard, convinced this will somehow lead to a breakthrough in understanding social cohesion. Meanwhile, we're all wondering if we can just go back to our labs and dissect something—anything—because at least then we'd have a clear outcome and not be left pondering the significance of our human chain's weak links.

What many professors fail to realize is that STEM students thrive on real-world applications. We want to know how sociological theories translate into practical solutions, much like how physics has led to technological advancements. Yet, when our professors insist on discussing the intricacies of social stratification without linking it back to the tech industry or engineering practices, we find ourselves adrift in a sea of jargon that feels utterly detached from our reality. It's like trying to relate the laws of thermodynamics to the social dynamics of a coffee shop—interesting in theory, but utterly useless when you're trying to finish a project on time and caffeinate simultaneously.

Ultimately, the impact of these professors on STEM student engagement is a curious case of mismatched expectations. While they strive to infuse their lectures with the rigor of scientific inquiry, they often lose the very essence of what makes sociology compelling: its relevance to human experience. Instead of fostering a genuine interest in social structures, they inadvertently create a chasm between the disciplines, leaving STEM students to groan in unison at the thought of navigating the murky waters of sociology. If only these professors could learn to appreciate the beauty of a good experiment in its own right, perhaps they'd discover that sociology, much like a well-executed lab procedure, has its own set of rules—and, more importantly, its own kind of fun.

The Art of Making Sociology Seem Like Rocket Science

Welcome to the world of sociology, where the only thing that might explode is your brain trying to comprehend why people act the way they do—without a single equation in sight. For STEM students, the challenge lies not in the complexity of rocket science, but in surviving the seemingly simple concept that humans might do things just because they feel like it. If only people came with user manuals, right? Instead, you're handed a textbook that reads like a philosophical treatise on why your neighbor leaves their Christmas lights up year-round. No wonder STEM students groan at Sociology 101; it feels like trying to solve a differential equation while navigating a maze blindfolded.

Learning styles play a pivotal role in this sociological comedy of errors. STEM students are trained to tackle problems with logic and precision, much like a scientist calibrating a rocket engine. Yet, sociology asks them to embrace chaos and emotion, leading to a perpetual state of cognitive dissonance. Imagine being told to build a bridge using spaghetti while simultaneously analyzing the social dynamics of why people prefer pizza over tacos. It's as if the universe decided to throw a curveball, leaving students wondering if they enrolled in the wrong course. Perhaps if sociology were framed as an elaborate experiment in human behavior—like watching a reality TV show—they might find it more palatable.

Speaking of reality, let's explore the real-world applications of sociology for our STEM majors. Imagine a sociological study on why engineers are notoriously bad at social gatherings. Armed with statistical analysis, students could present their findings at conferences, using their scientific prowess to explain the correlation between introversion and a strong affinity for power tools. This approach could transform the course into an engaging platform for students to observe their peers' interactions, akin to a live-action experiment. If only they could launch a survey on the best snacks for sustaining energy during long study sessions while maintaining focus on the intricacies of human relationships—now that's a project worth pursuing.

Ah, the language barrier. The moment STEM students encounter terms like "cultural hegemony" or "symbolic interactionism," they might as well be reading ancient hieroglyphics. The terminology differences between STEM and sociology can feel like switching from a language that is precise and concise to one that revels in ambiguity and nuance. It's a classic case of "Lost in Translation," where students are left scratching their heads, wondering if the professor is discussing human behavior or just ranting about the latest episode of a soap opera. A sociologist's use of metaphor can be as baffling as a rocket scientist discussing the intricacies of propulsion without ever mentioning thrust.

To keep STEM students engaged in sociology, faculty must adopt creative teaching strategies that resonate with their scientific minds. Picture this: instead of dry lectures, professors transform the classroom into a think tank, hosting debates where students analyze social phenomena with the same fervor they would apply to algorithm challenges. Incorporating technology, hands-on activities, and real-time data analysis can turn theory into practice, making sociology feel less like a chore and more like a thrilling lab experiment. Who needs a rocket to the moon when you can launch a discussion on social media's impact on communication trends? With the right approach, sociology can become an adventure rather than a dreaded requirement, turning groans into laughter and confusion into curiosity.

Conclusion:

In conclusion, this book serves as a humorous—and occasionally absurd—reminder that terminology matters. The terms that sociologists and STEM professionals use to describe the world are not simply different, they are fundamentally different ways of seeing the world. A sociologist might see the world through the lens of social structures, norms, and socially constructed realities, while an engineer or scientist might be more concerned with objective data, physical laws, and measurable constructs. This book has explored how these differences in perspective can lead to both productive collaborations and head-scratching misunderstandings, especially when terms like "social construct" pop up in places where they simply don't belong—like engineering meetings.

We've laughed, we've pondered, and hopefully, we've come to appreciate the complexity and humor inherent in the language barriers that exist between disciplines. The takeaway here isn't that one field is more important than the other, but that they each have their own set of rules, language, and constructs that should be respected—even if they seem utterly ridiculous at times. So, the next time you hear a sociologist talk about race as a social construct, or an engineer complain about the lack of concrete definitions, remember: they're speaking different languages—but perhaps they could use a bit more humor in their cross-disciplinary conversations.

Disclaimer:

This book is written as a satirical exploration of the sometimes bewildering differences in terminology between STEM disciplines and sociology. The content within is not meant to discredit or belittle either field—far from it. Rather, it highlights the playful absurdity that arises when concepts from one world are applied in the other without translation.

The terms and situations discussed in this book are exaggerated for comedic effect, and should not be taken as accurate representations of the fields involved. No sociologists were harmed in the making of this book, and engineers, well, they've been adequately warned. The aim here is to entertain, provoke thought, and, perhaps, open up space for a more humorous dialogue between two distinct ways of thinking. Remember, this is satire—just like race is a social construct, this content is a literary construct meant to amuse, not to inform in the traditional sense.

Please read with an open mind and a sense of humor, and enjoy the satire as it bridges the divide between two often contradictory worlds!

Printed in Great Britain
by Amazon